Killer View

Jim Warren was looking for a place with a spectacular view to build a home for him and his teenage children.

He found the perfect place, near Pavon! He took some pictures and was leaving when he thought he heard a shot.

The next morning there was an item on the news about a body, shot through the head, found on a local property. The camera showed the double waterfall from a slightly closer angle.

Then he downloaded his digital camera and looked at the pictures. There was something in two of them, when he blew them up, he hadn't noticed, at the time.

A man with a rifle.

Killer View
© 2013 & 2020 by C. D. Moulton
all rights reserved: no part of this publication may be reproduced or transmitted in any form or by any means, electronic or mechanical, including photocopy, recording, or any other information retrieval system, without permission in writing from the copyright holder/ publisher, except in the case of brief quotations embodied in critical articles or reviews.

This is a work of fiction. Any resemblances to persons, living or dead, or events is purely coincidental unless otherwise stated.

Contents

About the author

CD Moulton has traveled extensively over much of the world both in the music business, where he was a rock guitarist, songwriter and arranger and in an import/export business. He has been everything from a bar owner to auto salvage (junkyard) manager, longshoreman to high steel worker, orchid grower to landscaper, tropical fish farmer to commercial fisherman. He started writing books in 1983 and has published more than 350 books as of January 1, 2023. His most popular books to date are about research with orchids, though much of his science fiction and fantasy work has proven popular. He wrote the CD Grimes, PI series, and the Det. Nick Storie series, Clint Faraday series, and many other works.

He now resides in Gualaca, Chiriqui, Panamá, where he writes books, plays music with friends, does research with orchids and medicinal plants. He has lately become involved in fighting for the rights of the indigenous people, who are among his closest friends, and in fighting the extreme corruption in the courts and police in Panamá.

He offers the free e-book, *Fading Paradise*, that explains what he has been through because of the corruption.

CD is the discoverer of the Chadam Protocol for curing cancer.

Facebook page Ambrosia peruviana for cancer.

Killer View

<u>*A Place in Paradise*</u>

Jim Warren looked out over the mountainside toward the Pacific. It was a magnificent view. This might just be the place for him and his wife. He had enough of the states and their ridiculously stupid economic policies. He could hope to get something to do here in Panamá. He didn't need the money, but would go crazy with nothing to do. There were good opportunities everywhere he looked for a designer of computer programs. It didn't matter where you were in the world. in that business.

So far, Panamá had proven a paradise for him. He didn't realize how far the states had drifted from freedom until he got out to where he could look back. The things that had seemed vital in importance to him only two months ago were just plain silly now.

He stopped the car to take a few pictures of the view. There was a sign just a little way back that said "se vende". For sale.

He would look further. This was the third place with a view that would equal anything he'd seen anywhere. Any one would be a great place for a home. Millie, his wife, would agree with him on any of them. It would be the perfect place to raise his fourteen year old son and sixteen year old daughter.

He stayed a few minutes longer, gazing over the expanse of lower land gently sloping down to the Pacific he estimated to be 30 miles away. He was at around a thousand meters elevation. This was like looking out the window in a plane. There were a couple of misty clouds below him to the right. It was a dream scene.

"What a great view!" he mumbled. "Just picture waking up and coming out on the porch for my coffee in the morning. Imagine the sunsets!"

He got back inside the car to move on around the mountain. He was soon between two, this one seaward. The road curved around the mountain. and he was heading almost opposite the direction he was coming.

Those lush jungles across a valley that was a huge cow pasture with clumps of trees spotted all over. It was beautiful beyond what he thought existed, except in computer modified photographs in travel magazines. He couldn't think of one of those he'd seen that would begin to compare to this reality. He had used the expression "achingly beautiful" before. Now he knew what it meant! Exactly!

There was a very good road along the mountainside, with that magnificent view across the valley. He was the only person anywhere close along here. He hadn't seen another car in the past fifteen or more minutes.

He went around a gentle curve and saw a thin waterfall across the valley. It was partly hidden in the lush forest. He stopped to take several pictures. His camera had a four gig memory that would store a thousand pictures at maximum resolution. If he kept finding scenes like this, he would have to use the second chip!

He glanced ahead, and gasped. There were two waterfalls in a cleft that ran together to form one about two thirds of the way down. It was a drop of several hundred meters, and literally took his breath away. He immediately stopped the car and started taking pictures. He moved about a hundred meters farther along, stopped again, then repeated that.

"God! What a killer view! I never knew anything like this existed! This is *it*! I don't care what it costs, I have to have a place right along here. What a *killer* view! I can raise a little over a million. I know I can get a hectare along here. Right here.

I'll give you a million dollars for a hectare, right here!

"God! There's a sign ... se vende. It says sixty hectares. I wonder if they'll break it up? I'll give you one million dollars for a hectare, right here! God! What a killer view!"

He called the number on the sign, and was told the gentleman who owned the place, Sr. Rojelio Rodriguez, would be available in about two hours or so. Feel free to go onto the property.

His Spanish was good. He asked how much per hectare. He was told the parcel couldn't be broken up, at all. The selling price was seven hundred fifty thousand dollars.

He almost, as the saying goes, pissed in his pants! The whole side with that fantastic view for less than he would have been willing to pay for one hectare, anywhere in the place!

He almost yelled, "Sold!" but knew that would be stupid beyond belief. The price would go skyhigh to where he'd have to pay the million for one hectare. He said, "Well, it's very nice, and far enough away from cities to where I can probably get some peace. I don't know. How about if I ask the wife if she would like this kind of place? She's from Wisconsin, in the states, and was raised on a dairy farm. This is cattle country.

"Tell you what. How about I get in touch with her on the computer this evening, and send her some pictures? We'll leave it up to her if she wants this or a place closer to what she calls civilization and I call polluted noise."

He could see her getting a greedy gleam in her eye. He'd talked to enough agents here to know what she would say now;

"Well, we have several people who say they are interested. We will have to see if they will up the buying price. That's the way all property is sold here."

"I understand. I can get that place in Bocas, right on the water for about the same price, and that's much more to my personal liking. I just thought I'd see if the wife would prefer this. It's sort of nice, and she doesn't care too much for the water. Wisconsin, you know.

"I'll call you tomorrow, or sometime, if she's interested. If you don't hear from me, she isn't."

"Oh! Well, I'll check and see if your offer to pay the asking price is acceptable. I have to admit the others are trying to get the price down. It's a lot of money."

"It's exactly what I'm willing and able to spend, seeing we're both admitting things. I want two fifty to build a house and so forth, so that will take the money I've set aside. I'll also admit I was looking for something a little smaller and cheaper, but she likes the cattle thing. I'll see what she says. Call you tomorrow? That is, if she makes up her mind that fast. Sometimes she does, sometimes she doesn't."

"I'll be waiting for your call, Mr. ...?"

"Warren. Jim Warren."

"I'm Ami Baez, no relation to Joan."

"Joan?"

"The famous singer. In the states."

"Oh, yes. Hippie era. I'll see what she says, and call you in the morning, sometime." He rang off.

"Yes! A killer deal for a killer view! I can't believe my luck! I really will raise cows. It'll bring in some money, and I won't be tied to contracts and demands on my time, so much."

He took some more pictures and got in his car as he heard a gunshot in the valley below.

"I hope I'm not going to be bothered with any hunters wanting to cross my property. The answer will be a resounding *no*!

"I've got to stop talking to myself."

He drove back toward the hotel, slowly, thinking how much more ordinary the spots he had seen before had suddenly become. He stopped once to look at the Pacific, and noted that he had come around the mountain. "His" property went to the top. He could also see the Pacific Ocean from there. It was altogether possible he could build a house on that ridgetop and would have two magnificent views!

He didn't even get P.O.ed when he had to wait so long at a checkpoint.

He was going to spend half the night down-loading all those pictures. The last fifty or so would go into a special file.

It was a little past two AM. He had finally down-loaded and sorted three hundred sixty two photos, and had them in separate files.

He decided to see what the day's news was. He flipped on the TV, and went to the news, TVN. There was a wreck where a truck hit a school bus. Six students injured, not seriously. The rains in Bocas were causing some problems. A body had been found near Pavón. A protest in Los Santos.

"His" land was near Pavón. He still had the computer on. He went to the net to check on the death.

The body of a young man from Boquerón was found just at dusk when Rojelio Rodriguez, the owner of the property on which the body was found, was putting his cattle in the milking barn. Jorge Bonitos had been shot through the head. The police are investigating at this time and will keep TVN informed as to progress.

Rojelio Rodriguez? Wasn't that the man who owned the property? The body was found on that property? Hadn't he heard a shot, just as he was leaving?

He tried to remember anything that might help the police. After all, he was right there!

Taking pictures. He couldn't remember seeing anything out of the ordinary, then, but he was concentrating on the view, and might have missed seeing something in the background. Or foreground.

His eyes wouldn't take anymore stressing tonight. He'd go through the photos in the morning. It would give him something to stop the nervous jitters and wanting to call Baez too early. He *must not* appear too anxious!

He turned the TV off, and went to bed.

Warren got up earlier than usual. He wanted to make a phone call! Right now! He knew that would be the ultimate stupidity, not to mention, Baez wouldn't be up at any 4:15AM.

He plugged in the coffee maker and waited, then called to have the kitchen send up huevos revueltos and hojaldres, with two bolitas.

He sighed and looked at the dark window, then turned on the computer. He went to TVN, but only the same bulletin was there. He was going to call Millie on Skype, but it was the same hour there, in Hilton Head.

Might as well check those photos in the file he'd labeled "My paradise" to see if there was anything that could be useful to the police.

He looked at the first ones, carefully, the ones from just before the place he was going to buy. Actually, the fence was just before that, so it was on "his" place, too!

Nothing that stuck out, so he went to the next series. There was a photo, the seventh in the series, that had a small spot of blue under a tree he didn't remember. That made him remember a like spot of blue in the second shot from the original series.

Those two were all that were there. He copied them to Documents, then went to Irfanview to blow them up. They were at 3860 X 2582 pixels, so would keep clarity for a lot of magnification.

First resizing didn't show much more, except that it appeared to be someone with a blue shirt and brown pants. It was from the back, and no details came out.

He went to the second. Same thing. Both shots were from the rear. The person was heading away from him. The first showed him at a little clump of trees before a rivulet, the second under another clump of trees, across the rivulet. The focus was on the waterfalls, so these were much closer, and below him.

The time on the first was 2:23PM. The second was 2:47PM. The distance between the clumps of trees was, he estimated, about thirty five meters or so. Whoever it was had stopped at the first or second place – or at both.

He brought up the magnification to maximum before the picture started to pixelate. The first one didn't show anything. The second showed the figure had a rifle seated on the branch of one of the trees.

"Oh, fucking shit!" he exclaimed. "Boy! Was *that* a killer view! Or view of a killer."

He called the police to say he had a picture of the killer in Pavón. It didn't show much, except a man of average everything with a rifle seated on a branch. It was taken about half an hour before the shot was fired. He then had to explain. He promised to bring copies of the photos to the station.

"We'll come there. We can bring a CD and can get official copies. From what you say, there's no original. You deleted the camera memory when you downloaded."

"Yes. I didn't have a clue that anything would be in those pictures before hearing the news last night – this morning, actually – and I had already downloaded and sorted the photos."

"This is important. Do you know the resolution you used in taking the pictures? Is your camera more than eight megs?"

"It's eleven point five megs. Thirty eight sixty by twenty five eight two."

"You mean something's going to go right on this? That will allow a lot of amplification, and we have a technician here who can even sharpen a photo that's in bad shape. What type of monitor on your computer? Donaldo is right here. He's the technician."

"Laptop. Dell. Less than a year old. Top of the line."

"Naldo wants to know if he can use it to resolve the pictures? You have much better equipment than ours."

"Sure!"

"Mr. Warren, I'll be there very quickly. This is a break like we almost never get!"

Jim hung up, and said, "To hell with it!" and called Millie. She said she had one of her psychic things, and knew he was going to call her. She woke up five minutes ago, and came in to turn on the computer.

He told her he found a paradise she was not going to believe. It was about one sixtieth what he was willing to pay for it. He would send her pictures, right away, including the ones of the murderer.

"Murderer? What have you gotten into now, James Warren?!"

"An accident. I'll tell you about it. I have to send the pics fast, because the police want to use my laptop."

"You end up in the damnedest situations!"

He talked while he sent the picture file. He rang off when the police knocked at his door. He invited them in.

Detective Santo Bandera introduced himself and Donaldo Martin. He brought the pictures up, and Naldo, as they called Donaldo, put a CD into the burner. He copied the photos and put them on split screen. Jim showed them the two small blue spots. Naldo wrote something on his pad and started typing. "This will bring out the highest resolution without distortion or pixelation," he explained.

He typed in some more, swore, then took a CD from his carrycase and installed a program to manipulate the photo, which was much larger and clearer than Jim could do. It showed the lower part of the left side of the face.

"What this does is take a formula from the size of the person and the structure of the bones we can see, and we can revolve ... about ten degrees. That's pretty good. Now let's see how much more ... we don't have the nose or eyes, but ... about this much." The face turned just a little more.

"Holy Mary!" Santo cried. "It's Bonitos! What the hell?!"

He took a photo of a man with blood smeared down the side of the obviously dead face from an envelope. The part of the face in Jim's photo matched the same part in Santos' photo. Exactly.

"Bonitos was shot with a three ought six. We got the slug out of a tree behind him. It makes a small hole that doesn't bleed too much."

"Now we do have a puzzle," Naldo said. "It would appear Bonitos supplied his own murder weapon."

"I don't think so!" Jim cried. "Bring up that rifle as close as you can."

Naldo moved the picture where the rifle was showing. It was a Remington 380.

"Then what the hell happened to that rifle? It wasn't there!" Santo said.

"As a guess, I'd say the killer has it, now," Jim answered. Both Naldo and Santo nodded grimly.

They soon copied all they wanted. They had the whole file Naldo could go over carefully with his maximum magnification program. They left, promising to keep Jim up to date with anything they discovered.

It was only ten twenty. He was *not* going to rush things with Baez. He was *not* going to show her he was as anxious as he was.

He thought a moment, then went back to check over all the other pictures he'd taken, particularly the ones before "His" place. He didn't expect to find anything, and didn't.

He forced himself to take a walk around the little park, then to eat a sandwich at a little restaurant. It was almost twelve. He started to take out his cell phone, put it back, and grinned. He walked around some more, and bought a few things he needed, then made the critical call at one fifteen.

"Snra. Baez? Jim Warren here. Sorry I didn't call earlier, but I had some pictures the police are interested in. About the dead body found on Sr. Rodriguez' place.

"Millie, my wife, is studying the pictures. She said she liked the look of the place, so far, but wants to see them all. I'll call you in a couple of hours, if that's okay."

"Mr. Warren ... pictures? The body?"

"Oh, that. I was taking pictures to show the wife and a man who turned out to be the dead man was in a couple. I didn't see him, at the time, but the police brought him out and identified him."

"I, er, see. I talked with Mr. Rodriguez, just fifteen minutes ago. He said to sell it to you if you want it. He was rather shaken up, finding the dead man, you see. If it weren't for that, he'd probably try to get people bidding against each other. You *did* offer what he was asking, so he'll settle for that.

"If I may say, Mr. Warren, we could keep the place another year, and get a million, I'm sure. This is a good deal for you."

"Okay. I'll try to get Millie to hurry up. I'll tell her we can always sell it if it's not quite what we want."

"Yes! You can tell her it's a very solid investment, if nothing else!"

"Yeah. I'll call you later, I guess. It may not be until the morning ... oh, hell! I have to go into David tomorrow!

"Well, I can come back the first of next week, I guess. I'd put a down on it if I didn't ... she's sort of fickle. I guess we can wait until next week, if we have to. I'll still probably be in the mood then."

"Er, Mr. Warren, if you will put a surety to guarantee you are serious, I'll see that it is held. It can be quite small, just to let Mr. Rodriguez know you are serious. I'll tell him I have to do that to guarantee the price to you, or you will look elsewhere for property. If that is suitable?"

YES!

"Oh, okay. I guess ... okay. A little bit to guarantee I'm serious. How about, oh, two thousand five? If Millie wants it, I can get you the rest within four ... make that ten days."

"Why, that will be wonderful!" she exclaimed. "Do you know where the office is?"

"Maybe we'd better do it at the bank. I'll have to get the money there, anyhow. BNP? I have to ... if I'm fast, I can get it ... I don't want to rush you, but I might have to go at any moment. Can you meet me there in, say, half an hour?"

"Done! I'll be there!"

He hung up, and danced a happy little jig. He had worked their system against them, and gotten a fair deal! Him, a gringo!

He got his identification and BNP bankbook and went to the bank. Ami Baez was already there, waiting. She was a rather attractive woman in her mid-thirties, and dressed well. They went into the little secure room in back with the bank manager where he gave her a bank check for two five and they both signed a contract that said he had thirty days to produce the rest of the money, whence-upon title for the property would revert in full to James Francis Warren. Baez thought she had tied him into the deal by being oh-so clever. He knew he'd tied her into the deal with her own method. He definitely had to be the biggest winner in that negotiation! He had sewed up title to a property worth, in his estimation, fifty time what he paid for it. He checked the plano, and saw it was quite a lot larger than he thought, but that was because he thought of acres instead of hectares. A hectare is 2.4 acres.

He went out, saying he just had time to make his appointment. He would return on Monday. Three days. He would either forfeit the deposit or pay the rest of the agreement.

He drove to a little town with a small hostel, and booked in. He had internet service, and called Millie to tell her what had happened. She said she could believe the place was the paradise he had described by the pictures. She was going to love it! She hoped the horses in the pictures came with the place. The kids and she loved to ride. 144 acres was a lot of land that could be made to produce a good living with the cattle.

He sacked out later that night in a state nearing ecstasy. He didn't think Santo had learned any-thing more. He would have called, and didn't.

In the morning, he got a call from Santo. He had been mentioned in the news story as a tourist who had taken pictures at the finca where the murder took place, and had shown them some valuable shots that could well help bring the case to a satisfactory and early resolution.

"We didn't leave a hint as to who you are. We can hope that someone will try to find out. That would be very telling, in itself. I wanted to tell you about it before you see it on the TV, to let you know you weren't – and won't be – identified."

"Did you find anything about what someone may have wanted to kill him for?"

"No. He seemed to be one of those people who don't have any serious enemies or friends. He liked the mercenary soldier idea – if the things in his house are an indication. It makes me wonder if he came upon some drug deal or something and was going to pull the big hero macho man act. That can be fatal as fast as anything you can do. Those are not people you want to fool around with. Ever."

"I damned sure don't! I hope you find out what it's about and get the killer. I hope my pictures showed you something more than what I found."

"Naldo says he may have found something, but it's difficult to bring out. You had a couple of pictures that showed a small piece of the river that determines the property line between the finca and the national land where the cascadas are. There was something there, but we can't be sure what. It may be an Indio cayuca. It is partly behind some trees, and is far away. It will pixelate when we magnify it, I'm afraid."

"I don't remember seeing anything on the river. That doesn't mean very much, because I didn't remember seeing Bonitos, either. My wife saw something that may mean something. Horses."

"Horses? There are four that are a part of the place. They show in your pictures."

"Four? I think I saw ... check all the pictures of horses! I'm sure there were five of them, because I noticed there were three brown quarterhorse type, together in a spot, one palomino, and one paint, in other spots. That's five. Find which horse doesn't belong there!"

"Palomino? Paint? All the horses of Rojelio are brown work horses."

"Then we have two that shouldn't be there, and I didn't get the fourth quarterhorse's picture."

"One. Some people saw Bonito on the road, riding a paint.

"You are quite certain there was a palomino?"

"Positive. My wife and two kids love horses, and have pictures all over the house."

"Then we are looking for someone who rides a palomino and has a Remington rifle, aren't we? We progress, if slowly."

Monday morning at ten fifteen, Jim returned to the town. He called Baez and said his wife was willing to take a chance that the place would suit both her and the kids. The kids were the deciding factor. He went with her to the bank, where Rojelio was waiting, and they closed the deal. He immediately went to the registro publico and had the title transferred to his name. The land was now his, free and clear.

He called Millie, and said to start packing. The kids would be out of school in three weeks for the summer. They would probably never want to go back to the states again.

He then went to a little restaurant for lunch. Baez and Rodriguez were there with a lanky GI Joe type, if he'd been a gringo. He smelled of horses. He was introduced as Manuel Gomez, called Manny.

"Manny says he was interested in you when Ami told him you were the one who took the pictures the police have," Rojelio said. "He says he wanted to buy that place for a long time, but didn't have the money. I think he wants you to sell him a little piece of it."

Jim almost reacted when he learned that Ami told anyone he was the one who took the pictures. He said it was far too soon for him to be thinking of selling anything, though he might, at some future date.

They chatted awhile. Manny twice tried to get him to tell them what the pictures the police had showed. He answered that he didn't really know much. Something about (He thought. Worth a try!) the horses, and somebody in a blue shirt.

"Horses?" Manny asked, looking, Jim thought, a little scared.

"Yeah. There were too many, or not enough, or something. I don't pretend to know what it's about. I was just looking at land, and took some pictures. I don't know how many of the horses are supposed to be there. I do want to know if any of them go with the place."

"There are four that go with the place. The cows do not," Rojelio said. "You may buy them, or some of them, or I will move them."

"My wife's parents raised cows, so maybe I'll buy them for her, if it's not over my budget."

"There are sixty three there. I will sell them all for twelve thousand dollars. It will save me the high expense of moving them and renting a pasture until I can sell them."

"Okay. I'll get the money for you tomorrow."

They chatted for a bit more, then went their separate ways, Jim to the police station.

"What do you know about a man called Manuel Gomez?" Jim asked.

"Gomez? He has a small finca where he raises a few horses and chickens."

"Baez told everyone I took the pictures. He was trying to pump me about them, and what you know."

"I see. That would quite possibly explain the palomino. He breeds them. Perhaps he was there, but I don't think he would kill anyone.

"The paint is back to Fredrico's finca. Bonitos was, indeed, using it. The saddle was on it, still. The gate by the river was left open, and the fourth horse of Rojelio was there.

"Ami tells me you have bought the property for cash. It is a very pretty place. You will continue to raise the cows?"

"Yes. My wife's parents were cattle farmers, in Wisconsin. She'll like the idea of being with livestock. These are raised for the beef, more than milk. That will be the only real difference.

"Have you found anymore about who may have killed Bonitos, and why?"

"No. We know that he, like a few others in the area, was a member of a home protection group. Gomez is in that. They are practicing over much of the province. They are planning to be prepared when the Chinese or USA invade Panamá."

"They're going to invade Panamá?"

"Since Noriega, I would not be very greatly surprised. I don't think there would be much difference if they did."

"Hah! Go to the US now, and see the difference a few years have made. You have freedom here. There is little in the states, anymore. China would worry me, because they're getting in control of a lot of the food supply. That's a serious weapon, in the cities. I think they would try for economic takeover rather than armed. Arms in this part of the world would be much too disastrous to China. Retaliation would be taken there.

"It does give me an idea, though. I'll see if I can find anything."

"It is something I should not pursue?"

"It could be too dangerous to you and to other people, if I'm right. I think it's a possibility, but a very small one."

Santo studied him a moment, and shrugged. "Be most careful."

"That, I can promise!"

He went back to the hotel, then to his lawyer to have the papers finalized. The lawyer chided him for not using the firm for the whole purchase, to ensure he wasn't cheated or taken advantage of. He didn't say what he thought of lawyers in general – and most local Panamanian lawyers, in particular. The way *not* to be cheated or taken advantage of was to avoid them anytime possible.

He asked, "Have you read *Fading Paradise*?"

"No. Why?"

"It shows that a lawyer or not doesn't have much effect. Handle what you can, yourself, and bring them in at the end to be sure the records are straight. Even then, there aren't any sure things. The laws here are slanted in favor of the crooks."

"And a great percentage of the lawyers here are the worst kinds of crooks. I know. It is something we good lawyers try to fight."

"Yet you have a bar association most people can't find, much less contact, and they aren't known to have ever acted to the advantage of the clients. Let's not get into the political doubletalk routine.

"If anyone, for any reason, contacts you, or asks questions about me, I want you to inform me, immediately. A man was recently murdered on that property, and I was taking pictures, at the time. I've already had some strange questions asked by some very strange people. I'm bringing my family here, and want them safe. I'm not flexible one degree, where my family's concerned. Make that a more than doubled warning if anybody politically connected asks anything. Understood?"

He considered a moment. "And the police?"

"I expect Santo to check. I gave him evidence. He has to be sure I'm not involved in anything that could taint the evidence."

"Not Santo. Not here."

"Then one of my questions is answered. It was a thing 'way back in the background that's now right smack in front of me!"

"I am becoming concerned about this. I must know what I am to face!"

"Nothing. It's not you. All you can tell them is what you know. Don't even try to know more than that I'm a client who retained your firm, two months ago, to handle any legal matters here in Panamá. You handled my residence papers and my land purchase."

"That *is* all I know!"

"Keep it that way!"

He nodded. Jim left.

So! A vague wonder that didn't even get to the suspicion stage was now the apparent fact.

Jim went back to the hotel to find a man in a suit there. A suit meant politician or lawyer.

"Mr. Warren? I'm Javier Xavier," he greeted. "I represent a group who may wish to come to a mutual agreement about the farm you purchased. We are milk producers. We might wish to form a partnership, whereunder we raise the cattle with more modern methods for greater production.

"I know this is very soon, but there are others. We try to be first with the best offer!"

"Let me see. You want to establish a modern milk production facility with my place and my cattle, right?"

"In a word."

"In a word, no. I raise beef cattle."

"We can bring in dual-purpose cattle. We can produce better beef, as well as better milk."

"Well, I understand that feeds laced with certain hormones and antibiotics can greatly increase production. It can be the difference in profit and loss."

"Exactly!"

"But I don't believe in medicating the public with these things that turn out to be deadly twenty years or so down the line, so the word is now emphatically no."

Xavier stared, and shook his head. "I fell face first right into that one. Without the chemicals?"

"Which would last two weeks to a month, then I'd be tied into it. No."

"How about...."

"What part of 'no' don't you understand?"

"What's up? This is too fast a rejection."

"Javier Xavier? Really? What part of the USA were you educated in? You don't quite get the false Spanish accent across. Why did you knock off Bonitos?"

"I don't have the least vague idea of what you're talking about. Puerto Rico. We didn't."

"I don't know. It was exactly like it looks. I was taking pictures of a piece of land I wanted to buy, did buy, and happened to be there at that time."

"Truth?"

"All the way."

"How did you figure me?"

"Come on! I'm not the brightest candle on the cake, but I'm not an idiot, either!"

He chuckled. "Will you agree to let me know if you learn anything more? This is important to the ... to a lot of people."

"What was he into – or was he working for you?"

"Don't know. Don't know."

"They're sending you guys out without a clue as to what you're there for, now? It figures."

"It's effective, sometimes. People say things that don't mean anything to me, I report, they mean something to somebody else."

"They gonna tell you and send you back, or send somebody else?"

"Probably." He grinned. Jim grinned back.

"Joe Fellows. Romney, West Virginia. I like you."

"I think you're okay. Jim Warren. You know all that about me.

"Should I keep my family in the states awhile?"

"They're not going to be bothered – by us. Neither are you. We'll probably keep an eye on you to see who else tries to contact you.

"Has anybody, yet?"

"Some cop from somewhere else contacted my lawyer, who doesn't know a damned thing, and won't. I know better than to let a Panamanian lawyer know more than my name, rank, and serial number."

He laughed. "Ain't that the truth! It applies to any lawyer, anywhere."

"Just about."

"Well, I guess I'll go report that you made me from the get-go. I'll probably also tell them we get along, so they'll keep me handy. I really do love this place. I hate to see it screwed up, but that's as much as inevitable."

"Sad, but true."

He stood, offered his hand, then left.

And I fell for that to the same degree I fell for the Javier Xavier crap! Jim thought. He went to his room, and looked around. He found the little transmitter microphone stuck to the back of a vase of artificial flowers.

He could maybe use that, if it came to wanting to misdirect someone. He'd leave it there, for the time being. Trouble might be that he didn't really know which side put it there. It didn't seem like that kind of thing a sophisticated agency would use.

Was he getting tangled into some kind of wild plot cooked up by the CIA, or one cooked up by some local weird-os?

It might be fun – but it might also be dangerous. He wasn't into international intrigue.

There simply couldn't be anything there in the middle of nowhere for any international attention. It was crazy! It was purely weird!

He called Millie, and chatted about the place and horses and cows. He would spend the entire day, tomorrow, going over the place. He wanted to know it, to experience it. Even all this mess didn't deter him from believing he had to be the luckiest person on the face of the earth to actually be able to own such a place!

He parked the Land Rover he was able to buy and opened the gate, drove in, and reclosed it. He stared for a few seconds at the magnificent view of those falls, then went to the clump of trees where Bonitos had stood with the rifle braced against the limb. There was nothing out of the ordinary there.

He went on toward the milk barn. There were three small Indio children there, he would guess five, six, and eight years old. He introduced himself. He learned they were Emilio, Carlos, and Basilio Smith.

"Smith?"

"It is a common name for Indigenos from the Bocas area," a very handsome Indio youth of about eighteen years said, coming in, leading a cow. "I am Balbino Smith, their uncle."

He told them to take the cow to the stall and milk it.

"I see. I didn't discuss with Rojelio about the people who work for the place."

"We work for percent. I take care of the cows, and I get what the milk brings. It is well for both of us, because I care for the animals, and he gets the money, when they are sold for meat."

"Do you live on the finca?"

"No. The one next (pointing). I come here every morning, and work on my land every afternoon. Basilio is in charge, and takes care of things after the noon meal. He is here some, and on our finca some. He was not here when the man was shot, but we heard the shot."

"But ... he's just a child!"

"I don't understand?"

"You said he is in charge, in the afternoon. He's a child!"

"I don't understand your gringo thought. He is a person. He has responsibilities. Without that, his life has no meaning."

"I've heard about the Indio philosophy. It seems to work a lot better than the screwed up mess we have! We'll have to have some long conversations."

"Then you will wish to continue the agreements with Rojelio?"

"Very definitely!"

"I think we will be friends. I must bring the last cow."

"You've milked all of them, already? It's not eight o'clock yet!"

"The truck comes in half an hour. The milk must be ready. We come at the first dawn. We will then see that there is feed for the pregnant cows. We will cut the poison weeds by the river.

"There are many good fish in the river. There are prawns.

"We will talk later. Coin dega!"

They had been speaking Spanish. "What is that? Coin dega?" Jim asked.

"It is our language. Good day."

"Coin dega to you!"

"Ahn mok coin dega!"

Jim waved, and went toward the river. Balbino was bringing in the last cow. Emilio was leading the one they had milked out to send it down to the pasture. A hard lump came into Jim's throat, and tears to his eyes. Perfect people in a perfect place, and he was there. He hadn't known he was capable of feeling anything as strongly as he felt now. Somehow, he didn't feel the place was "his." He felt it was "ours." He didn't know what that meant, but he would learn. This was nature as it was meant to be. The Indios were people as nature meant them to be, not enemies, but part of nature. He didn't understand that, either. He felt it.

He wandered around the property for more than an hour, and down to the river coming from the falls, that marked his property line. National land on the far side of the river. Natural and beautiful beyond imagination. A place he hoped would never change, make that *be* changed, in his lifetime. The cold water was crystal clear. All colors of smooth small rocks lined the bottom.

He moved on along the bank, and rounded a bend, where he heard laughter. There was a deeper pool under a little cascada that ran over some large brown boulders. The Smiths, plus two small girls, one about four, and the other maybe seven. Were swimming and playing in the cold water. They saw him, and waved for him to join them. They had stripped, and their clothes were folded and put on a flat rock in the sunlight.

He didn't even think about it. He stripped, folded his clothes, and joined them. The water seemed cold, at first, but he was soon comfortable. He played with the children, and dove from the boulder. He was standing on the boulder, ready to dive, when Balbino tackled him from behind. They both went into the icy water and wrestled like he had when he was fourteen, in the lake with friends. He felt he was totally accepted by these people.

After about half an hour, Balbino, now Bino, said play time was over. Work to do! They all climbed out of the water and laid around on the flat rock in the sun to dry. A beautiful woman came along the path, carrying a small baby. Jim didn't feel the least embarrassed for being nude, there. Bino introduced his wife and baby, Nilsa and Balbinito. They chatted until they were dry, then dressed and went their separate ways. He thought about his daughters in this society, and, strangely, wasn't much concerned. He knew they weren't sexually active, at home – no. Back up north. *This* was home, now – and that they would be, here, very quickly. It was part of the culture.

Weird! That thought would have driven him right up the wall in the states!

He walked to the road and up the mountain on the far side to the top. There was a flat mesa on top that was about sixty meters wide. It was fairly solid rock, and would be the perfect place for his house. He could look one way to see the blue Pacific on the horizon, the entrance road below him. The view turned around was of those waterfalls and the forests.

This was paradise. He didn't need to die to be in a heaven he didn't believe in. He was here and alive, more than he'd ever been before, and in it!

He stayed awhile, then went back down the path to the road and to his car. Basilio came to tell him a man had come on a horse, and wanted to come in. He wouldn't allow it unless Jim said it was alright.

An eight year old boy wouldn't allow an adult to come onto the property?

"What would you do if he came in, anyway?"

He shrugged. "I don't know. Call my uncle, I think."

"Do you know who the man was?"

"I think they call him Gomez. He has the pretty horses."

"Have you ever seen any of his horses here?"

He shrugged again. "I think so. They are pretty, but they are strong, too. They can work. If they come when it is breeding time, it would be a good match."

Very matter-of-fact.

Jim chatted with Basilio as Basilio checked all the water barrels and washed down the milking barn. Just at dusk, he went to his car and headed for the hotel. He cleaned up, had a good meal, and went to a little bar two streets away toward the "lower" side of town. He got some looks when he went in to order a cold beer. He seldom drank anything, but had heard that Balboa and Panama were good beers. They only had Atlas, which, so far as he knew, was a pretty good beer.

He started talking with a man. He said he had bought a place to build a house, nearby, so would probably be a regular. He wanted to know the local people. They said there were only a couple of gringos living in the near area. They were the snobbish type, and weren't popular.

"The type who say you should all learn English, because, after all, they are spending their money here?"

Jorge looked nervous, then laughed, and agreed that described them very well, thank you!

"I'm moving here to get away from that sordid type. I like the local people. The family next to my finca are very real people. I like real people, not these city-bred hybrids."

Several, who were listening, came to agree, and say they hoped he stayed. They needed someone, some rich gringo, to buy them beer!

"Beer, okay. Rum, no way!" he fired back, and bought a round for the bar. There were seven people there, and the bill came to six dollars ten cents. He stayed joking with them for three more beers, two of which they bought. He wasn't used to drinking, and was a little drunk and very happy when he went back to the hotel. Joe was in the lobby, and asked where he had been.

"Out. Why?"

"Just curious. I was ... watching you. No sense in lying. You went into the restaurant and came back out. I figured you would go to your car, and followed a minute later, but you were gone."

"I went to a little local bar."

"Not the lower side? That's dangerous!"

"Oh, bullshit! They're really great people! They're not dangerous because they won't learn English and cater to you rich snobs!"

"I guess I deserved that. It can be dangerous. You could get mugged."

"They're welcome to try. They might find not all gringos are soft and easy to intimidate."

"I suppose you won't tell me when you're going anywhere?"

"Fuck, no! It's none of your damned business!"

He laughed, at that. "I still like you. I suppose I wouldn't exactly appreciate being followed. You won't believe me, but it's for your protection."

"From what?"

"We don't know! It was just to keep a lid on things that he was in any ... we don't know what's happening here. We just don't want to take any chances."

"Seems silly."

"Seems a way to stay alive."

"I'm don't know anything, either. There would be no be any point in killing me. It could only make it worse for whoever."

"I hope they see it that way. We can't see any point to killing Bonitos. They did."

"Maybe it was personal? Maybe you and your organization aren't even involved?"

"Why would he carry that rifle in there, then?"

"Maybe it was personal? Maybe you and your organization aren't even involved?"

"I get the point. It's really the only way that figures."

"Or maybe he was playing both ends against the middle? I still wouldn't be involved."

"It's a weird situation."

"You like understatement, do you?"

That got him the finger.

Jim got up in the morning and decided to go to the police station to see what was new. He was feeling great. He knew there were things not so great about Panamá, but also knew he had found as close to paradise as was even possible for him, personally.

Santo said there wasn't much new. It seemed that the national records didn't have anything about Bonitos or Gomez.

"What about Javier Xavier?" he asked.

"You're kidding, right? Javier Xavier?"

"CIA. Real name, Joe Fellows, or so he said. They've probably cleaned the files of anything we might want."

"What's it about?"

"He says he doesn't know. He says they have no idea why Bonitos was killed, and they're very nervous about it.

"Was Bonitos in one of those paramilitary things? You have them here?"

"I don't know. That would be why the records would be purged by the USA. They back those kinds of things, then come to our aid when they don't turn out the way they'd planned. If he was, he was a CIA agent, and that's what they're so worried about."

"I think the one to check on is Gomez. He went to the finca, but Basilio wouldn't let him come in."

He laughed. "The little Indio kid? You have to take him seriously! He wouldn't let me in, either. I was going to go in, anyway, and he said I would be very sorry if I did that. He called his uncle to give him permission to let us in.

"I really do think he would have some way to make me very sorry, if I hadn't gotten permission. He was so serious about it!"

"His duty is to keep unauthorized people out. He takes his duty seriously."

"To the point he'll stand alone against the Policía Nacionál!"

"Santo, I love those people. The whole Smith family. They're down-to-Earth good people."

"Maybe. You don't have to deal with the side of them I do."

"No, but I understand them. You don't."

"That may be truer than I want to admit.

"What does your CIA man look like? I might be able to cause him a little grief."

Jim took out his Blackberry and scrolled to a few pictures he had surreptitiously taken of Javier/Joe. "He's probably hanging around outside, right now, waiting for me to come out. He makes no secret of the fact he's following me. I might be able to use that."

"He told you he was?"

"In a way, yes. I went to the Cantina Maria, and he lost me. He was worried, because it's the dangerous side of town."

"It is, but not in a way that you would have to worry much. Maybe someone would try to mug you, but you're big enough to handle that, I tend to think."

"I had a great time, and got drunk for the first time in fifteen years. Four lousy beers, and I was drunk!"

"Hadn't been drinking for a long time?"

"Fifteen years. You can figure why I stopped drinking."

He nodded, and grinned. They talked a bit more about the murder, then Jim went to the lawyer for his copies of the legal papers, and to the bank, to arrange for a direct deposit from the states. He had enough trouble when he first wanted to open an account that he didn't want to go through a lot more when the money was transferred. He would keep a small account in the states to be able to handle the deal when he sold the property he had there.

He called Millie to make more plans, then went to a contractor to build his house. He didn't like the way this one was acting, so went to another, who was almost as bad. He was about to give it up and go into David, where he knew a contractor who might be convinced to come out there, when he ran into Jorge, from the bar. He said, "What the hell!" and asked him if there was a contractor who wouldn't be trying to screw him over.

"My cousin works for Jaime Soldas. He says he treats them right, and does good work. He charges a lot, but he gets the work done a lot faster than anyone else, and it's what he said, not all the time adding things on."

He took Jim to the cluttered office. Jaime was like so many of the Panamanian people; amiable and eager to help. He made no bones about the fact he was going to make a profit on any work he did.

"I give a price that looks like too much, they give a cheap price. I make the house for what I said, they have to add five hundred for the extra cement, because they had figured it wrong, at first. They have to add two hundred, because pipe went up, and six hundred because the window frames went up, and a thousand because zinc went up. Now they cost more than me, then they have to wait either until it stops raining or it starts, and they have to wait for the block, and the zinc wasn't delivered when they promised. It will be a month more. You're moved into mine and are happy that it's exactly what I promised."

"How much for a house like this?" He handed him a basic plan he had drawn.

Jaime looked it over, and said he would have to change the stairway. There wasn't any head room as you went up. He showed with a ruler that the last six steps didn't have room above to go without bending double. He then said there was too much foundation for the garage, and it wasn't a good idea to make stepdowns in the foundation. Make the foundation deeper and one piece.

"You get temblors, in this area. It will crack where you have the divisions. It's also cheaper to do it my way."

In an hour his plans were better than he'd made them, and the full cost would be presented when Jaime had run everything down to the wholesaler. "I get a guaranteed price with a little deposit. I'll ask that you forward a bit, if you agree to what I want, so I can fix the price."

Jim said that would suit him fine.

"One other thing. I will not put the very large windows in the windward face of a house up there. Two times per year, there are very strong winds on those ridges. A piece of limb coming into a window at fifty kilometers per hour will shatter it.

The maximum size of a tempered glass window that would stand that force and the wind pressure would be about four feet by six feet.

"I can put windows that size, or I can ... that sala is very large. Take two meters from the face, and make a veranda. I can install a wire drop-down protector screen at the rail, and use the large windows. It is easy to make a switch that will drop the screens when the wind pressure reached, say, thirty kilometers per hour. I can make it so it will also raise the screen if the pressure drops to twenty kilometers per hour. I would want that verandah on my home for the view.

"That is called a great room. It can easily have a verandah, both front and rear. You can move the kitchen to the inner side, and can use the verandah for regular meals. The dining salon can be used for parties and such."

"Give me a ballpark figure for doing it that way, including all the permits, or whatever."

"It will be very expensive. I think two hundred thousand dollars, or a little more."

Jim looked at the plan and at the pictures from the spot. "I'll give you one hundred thousand, now, and the rest when we sign the contract. This is within the planned budget."

They agree. Jim would have the cash money delivered tomorrow early.

"Meet me at BNP at nine o'clock. We can sign the contract, and have the bank record it on the form for the certified check I can deposit. I will be able to start next Wednesday. I will finish the job I'm doing now on Tuesday, and can move the crew and equipment directly there, instead of to the warehouse."

"Done!"

Jim was in the mood for another jig. After Jaime got through pointing out the mistakes he'd made and added the verandahs, it was better than he'd thought possible.

Now he had to wait for the hammer to fall. He'd never had such an up in his life that didn't end suddenly in a plunge to new depths.

He went back to the hotel in very good spirits. Gomez was waiting there, sitting on the swing, talking with Joe.

"Hi, Joe! Why weren't you following me?" Jim asked Joe.

"Mainly because there's no sense in both of us following you," he answered. "We were talking about why he was following. It seems this is a screwed up mess from the first.

"Gomez, here, is a fellow agency man. He's doing the same things I was doing."

Jim remembered that Joe wouldn't know about the palomino. He put two and two together, then.

"Both of you, well, Bonitos and you, were infiltrating that silly paramilitary thing that has the chance of going exactly nowhere?" he asked Gomez, whose mouth dropped open.

"I thought you didn't know what it was about?! I thought...!" Gomez cried.

"No, you didn't. That's the whole problem, isn't it? Doing things without thinking?"

"What do you mean?" Joe asked.

Jim shrugged, and put his hand in his pocket, punched the speed dial on the Blackberry, where he had set it when he saw the two there. He pulled the hand out with the key to his room in it. Started to walk off, heard the phone answered where only he could hear, and turned back, to say, "Gomez, you overlook things. Joe, he isn't any CIA operative. He was there. What we found in the pictures was his palomino on the finca. It was in the background, below where Bonitos had the rifle on the limb, and in three other pictures.

"Gomez, I've thought you killed him ever since we found those pictures, and you suddenly were everywhere I looked. When I learned you were the head man (strictly a guess, but it scored!) in that stupidity, it didn't leave much room for doubt that you were, as we say, 'it!' I was just waiting for you to make the slip you made by telling Joe you were CIA."

"But ... but I am!" Gomez cried, as Santo slid to a stop at the end of the sidewalk into the hotel.

"Your friend, Joe's, not, though. We have ways to check that," Santo said. "Care to tell me the story, or do I charge both of you?" He reached to turn the Blackberry off and take the earphones out.

"Not much to tell," Gomez said. "I was there, but I was down by the river, talking with a ... member of the group. I heard the shot, and went up to the barn, saw Bonitos had bought it, and got out. I've been looking for whoever killed him, because it would have to be the one who was going to sell the group a half a million dollars worth of automatic weapons.

"I checked with the company. Fellows is an agent. He's working the same case, but from the Colombian end."

"So? Why isn't he in Colombia?" Santo asked.

"Because I followed a man here who was supposed to deliver the weapons. Works for the old Escobar group."

"You will give me the name and location of that person, and I will not detain you," Santo said.

"I can't do that!"

"Joseph Fellows, AKA Javier Xavier, I arrest you on a felony charge of aiding and abetting a murderer. You will come with me, walking, or you will come with me, in shackles, in the truck."

"Hey! You can't do that!"

"I can and I will!"

"I'd like to know who and where, myself," Gomez said. "I'd like to know ... Officer, give me five minutes, okay?"

He went into the hotel lobby and took a small computer from his pocket. He used it for a few minutes, and came back out. "The agency would also like to know where this Escobar character is."

"He's not an Escobar. He works, or used to work, for them!"

"Who? Where?" Santo demanded.

"The agency would also like to know why you didn't report that you were coming here, after contacting them, last night, saying you were in Cali."

Fellows looked at the floor. Jim tensed, and slapped down hard on his arm as he pulled a pistol from his belt in back. The shot went into the floor. Gomez decked him.

"Well! Can I get some sleep now? I'm starting to build my house, and need some rest!" Jim said.

"You have to fill out the forms," Santo replied. "It shouldn't take more than six or eight hours."

"It would have been easier if you, as merely some schnook who happened to be here, had killed him!" Gomez said. "Now I'll have to fill out the forms, too!"

"Fuck you!" Jim cried, giving him the finger.

They laughed and joked a bit as they dumped the still unconscious Fellows into the back of the police truck. Gomez would ride back there with him.

When they got to the station, neither was in the truck. They hadn't stopped, and had only slowed once, to turn a corner.

"What the hell?!" Jim cried.

"I saw them jump out in the rearview mirror. I felt tonight wouldn't be a good time to spend filling out forms. I want to see where they go, and what they do."

"I never know what the hell's going on, anymore! Cripes!"

"I'll let you know when I know. You're out of it, from this point."

Jim said he wasn't filling out forms about an arrest that never was completed, and went back to the hotel. Santo would contact him as soon as anything more happened. It would be handled by the CIA, probably. Santo felt they would find a way to excuse Fellows for killing Bonitos.

Wednesday, Jim went to the finca, and was surprised to find the entire crew working on digging the foundation. He didn't think they would do anything the first day but mark out the areas to be dug.

"Why?" Jaime asked. "We mark out this side and the corner, then don't do anything while we mark the rest? The crew is supposed to stand around and drink coffee while three of us do the marking, then come back tomorrow, and the three of us stand around while the others dig?

"I can see that you will never be successful in business, here! You are not thinking in this world we inhabit."

Jim laughed. "I'm not used to being practical in Panamá. It doesn't fit, somehow."

Basilio and Emilio came up a little later to hug him and call him "Uncle Jim" (Tio Jim). They talked with the crew, asking a lot of questions. It was obvious the questions were serious. At one point, Basilio said that the wind would be bad for windows facing the ocean. Two times a year.

Eight years old, and knows about wind force!

"We have a safe screen that will drop from the Verandah rail," Jaime explained. Basilio nodded, wisely. Soon, he and Emilio hugged Jim goodbye and returned to their duties. Later, Balbino came to hug him and call him "brother" (hermano), and to say Nilsa had fixed lunch for him. She would bring it to the milking barn.

He went to the barn for a delicious lunch of chicken and rice and frijoles, with a salad made of vegetables he didn't know, and bananas fried with a little honey. They went swimming (Jim learned very quickly that the Indigenos were almost obsessively clean people. He was about to return to the house site, then reconsidered.

"Bino, they don't want me around while they're building, do they? Why?"

"They know you do things differently in the US. They feel you don't like what they're doing. They are waiting for you to complain about unimportant things."

"They're doing a great job! I have nothing to complain about!"

"That is not their experience with gringos."

He thought a minute. "I guess I'll go back to town. I won't be able to not come every day to take pictures of the progress."

"You take a lot of pictures. Tell them why you are doing that. They think you may want to find something wrong."

"Thanks, brother. I will." He hugged them all goodbye, and went back to take a couple more pictures. He told Jaime he wanted a record of everything to show people that they did a better job in Panamá than in the states.

"Better?"

"Yes. It's stronger, and will stand a temblor. In the states, it would crack, and have to be repaired.

What it boils down to is that you're building 'way over code."

He had to explain the code. They had one here, but knew it wasn't right, from experience. They built to a better code.

"Wait until the electric! You'll know it is true that some things are not done right!"

"I'm a qualified electrician. I can show you the best shortcuts. I'll guarantee this house will be over code, there!"

"You will teach my man?"

"If you like. It's not difficult."

He came every day, and did show the man Jaime wanted to train about electric the things he had to know. The man, Laro, made charts, and carefully wrote down what was needed. Things like, "Number fourteen is not good for cocina. Use twelve." "Romex cable can be put in the holder clips, and does not need to be in conduit." "Always use all three wires. If not grounded can cause dangerous shock." "Wire nuts and bronze cable connectors are second to solder. Do not use wire nuts on Chinesae wire, because it is an alloy that will not remain tightly connected." "Twist and tape not good. Not safe." "Do not splice cable side by side. Make one long and one medium and one short. Will not short if scraped bare." "Always ground metal switch/ plug boxes third wire." once he got a lesson, himself, he had Laro write down. There was a rain coming, but they were inside. He was showing how to connect a two-way switch when he got a shock that almost knocked him off his feet. He had Laro write, "Never be idiot enough to work with bare electrical wires during a thunderstorm!!!!"

Then the house was done. Millie and the kids would fly into David the day after tomorrow.

<u>Finally! Paradise!</u>

Millie and the kids got off the plane, and ran to hug him and exchange excited greetings. He held Millie a long time, then went to the Land Rover with their luggage. The big container of their furnishings and such would arrive in four days. They would stay in the hotel until it was there, though the kids wanted to stay at the house. They could use their bedrolls, and the kitchen was built in. Jim was about to say, "No way, José!" and thought.

"Whatever you want. Wait until you see the place! The pictures don't begin to do it justice!"

"Those pictures! I want to know who that *gorgeous* man is that works for you!" Sally, his daughter said.

"The gorgeous man who works for me? No gorgeous man works for me."

"You called him Bino, I think," Millie said. "He *is* gorgeous! I think you'll have to watch Sally like a hawk!"

"He doesn't work for me. He works with me. You'll find there's a difference. He's married, and has a new baby. His wife, Nilsa, is a beautiful woman. His nephews work with us."

"Nephews? Not those little children, surely!" Millie cried.

"Oh? Why not? They have their duties and responsibilities, in the Indio family. As Bino says, without that, they don't have a purpose, and will grow up never knowing where they belong.

"I'm really into the Indio philosophy."

"We were beside an Indio family on the bus, in Panamá City, last night," Sally said. "They had a baby and a little boy, about four. There were several children on the bus, and a couple of babies that howled the whole trip. The kids ran around, driving the parents crazy. The Indio baby didn't cry once, and the little boy stayed with the parents, and looked at the kids his age going crazy and didn't seem to understand how anyone could act that way."

"The Indio children are secure. None of the others are."

"What does that mean?" John, his son asked.

"You have to experience it. You can't explain it and make much sense."

They got to the road below with the distant view of the Pacific Ocean. They knew it from the pictures, but this was real, and better.

They came near the bend around the mountain, and saw the house on top. "I'll settle for a house like that!" Millie exclaimed. "What a view they must have! Oh, please, Jim! Tell me we have something with a view half as good as that one has!"

"I suppose it probably does, seeing that's our house!"

"Oh, God!" Sally cried. "Don't be lying! Don't be that cruel!"

Jim grinned. They went around the mountain, and came on the view of the waterfalls. He drove into the finca, and to the milk barn, where Basilio came out to hug Jim and greet them all. He stared at Sally with her long blond hair, and said she was beautiful.

"Uncle Jim, I will call to the others now. They will come. Wait, please?"

"Of course. I want our family to all know each other."

He made the Indio "Oye!" call, and was soon answered. He called "They are here!" in the Indio dialect.

A few minutes later, the children came running up to hug "Uncle Jim" and meet the others. Nilsa and Bino came in soon to hug him and call him brother. He held to them, and introduced his family. Sally looked like she would faint. Bino had been working, and didn't have on a shirt. He was an exceedingly handsome man, Jim noted, for the umpteenth time.

They all almost danced across the road and up the path to the house. As they were crossing the road, two Indio youths about seventeen years old were passing. Bino introduced Nicanor and Cano. They were very much like Bino. Sally looked like she would faint, again.

John whispered to Jim, "She ain't gonna be a virgin this time next week!" Jim surprised himself, and laughed.

They went on to the house. The kids wanted to stay there tonight. None of them could experience enough of the views. Millie got Jim aside, and asked him what they should do about Sally. She was worried if she stayed up there without their supervision.

"This isn't the states, Hon," Jim said. "You'll change your ideas about a lot of things. I think we've raised our kids right. I'm not worried."

"But she isn't experienced with sex! She's in heat, right now!

"I can't believe I'm saying this! I can just say I know how she feels, believe me! They are, as she said, *gorgeous*!"

"You've taught her about having safe sex, and protection, and all that?"

"Certainly."

"Then don't worry. This is paradise. Let her find hers. John will go crazy for the women. They're exotic."

She laughed. "You sure held Bino a long time with that hug. Maybe you know how we feel about him?" she grinned impishly.

"It's nice. We're brothers. The Indios touch a lot, and it's natural for them to hold each other. They communicate a lot by touch. You'll learn that. You'll learn how pleasant it feels to have Bino holding you. It's warm and wonderful. I've learned how it feels to have Nilsa hold me, the same way. It's warm and wonderful, and doesn't go beyond that."

"I can't believe we're having this conversation! I'm going to let my daughter ... this is unreal!"

"This place and these people affect the way you think about things.

"Where have the kids gotten to?"

They were on the verandah, chattering with the kids and Nilsa. Their highschool Spanish wasn't good, but they seemed able to communicate.

"Well, Millie and I will get back to town. We'll be here in the morning, and bring things for lunch. I want to introduce her to friends in a dangerous little bar."

"Dangerous?" she asked.

"So I'm told. It's dangerous in that I tend to get drunk after two beers, and they insist on buying more than that."

They said their goodbyes, and went back to the Land Rover. Millie looked up at the house and across to the waterfalls. There were tears on her cheeks.

"Oh, Jim. I'm finally here, in paradise!"

They were back at the hotel and cleaned up. Millie was a little worried about Sally, but also resigned to the fact their little virgin daughter was a woman now. She had to make her own choices.

They had dinner at the restaurant, and went to the little bar. Millie was a big hit. She was blond, in a place where there were almost never any blondes. When they went back to the hotel she said she couldn't remember when she had so much fun, or when she had made friends so fast. Back in the states, she wouldn't have been in any such bar, and wouldn't talk to people in any such fashion. This really was paradise.

They were getting into bed when the phone rang. It was Santo. He said he wanted to welcome the family.

"And one other thing," he finished. "Gomez called me. It seems Fellows had sold out to the group in Cali, Colombia. He had a hidden bank account they found, with over two million dollars.

He admitted he was contracted to break up the CIA connection with the paramilitary group, and felt the best way was to get rid of the person negotiating for the weapons and expose Fellows in the process. His heading the group meant it would fall apart because of mistrust of the CIA. Other than that, what does the family think of your killer view?"

"Don't call it that."

C. D. Moulton's works are available on most major outlets as printed or e-books. CD writes the CD Grimes, PI mysteries, the Det. Lt. Nick Storie mysteries, the Clint Faraday mysteries, the Flight of the Maita science fiction series, books on orchid culture and many others of many types. Mystery, adventure, intrigue, science fiction, fantasy, paranormal, mild erotica, and factual.